I0615231

S.M.X.

Grandma's Stories and Anecdotes

S.M.X.

Grandma's Stories and Anecdotes

ISBN/EAN: 9783744750448

Printed in Europe, USA, Canada, Australia, Japan

Cover: Foto ©Andreas Hilbeck / pixelio.de

More available books at **www.hansebooks.com**

GRANDMA'S
Stories and Anecdotes

OF

"YE OLDEN TIMES."

Incidents of the War of Independence, Etc.

BY

S. M. X.

Of the Visitation Academy, Baltimore, Md.

BOSTON:
ANGEL GUARDIAN PRESS,
1898.

INTRODUCTION.

THERE is a charm in a well-told story that few other things in life seem to possess; for children especially, it is the most engaging pastime. They will readily leave an interesting game and listen for hours to tales of adventure, historical anecdotes, or incidents of real life. Unfortunately, all well-told stories are not equally productive of benefit. Some, while they recreate and interest the child, convey to the mind nothing to improve it, or that cultivates the intellect.

Children's minds are as impressible as wax, with this difference; the image may be effaced from the wax, but from the memory, seldom or never; careful, then, should we be in our selection of stories for the little ones, remembering the adage of old: "Early impressions are lasting."

As the tree is easily bent when a sapling, so can the tender minds of children be inclined to good or evil by the nursery teachings. Too much care cannot be taken to impress them with a love of what will render them virtuous and happy in after life. Stories that convey the moral of truthfulness, uprightness and strict adherence to duty, can never fail to produce a lasting effect. Fiction is good but truth is more desirable. The contents of this little volume are founded on fact, and given in the simple language we caught up from the venerated grandma of years long since gone by; we fondly trust they may prove useful and recreative to the little lovers of tales and stories.

Baltimore, 1899

CONTENTS.

Grandma's Stories and Anecdotes

OF

"YE OLDEN TIMES."

PART I.

THE STAMP ACT AND TAXATION OF THE COLONIES.

THERE was no greater pleasure or treat for us than to gather around our dear old grandma in the long winter-evenings and listen to the stories of what she called "Ye Good Olden Times." She had many of the quaint sayings of old England that rendered her anecdotes and histories the more interesting.

Grandma was a remarkable personage; at the advanced age of eighty and more, her faculties were unimpaired and it was only the bent form that indicated decline of years and made us realize that the shades of night were fast gathering around the life that had been but sunshine and happiness to others for nearly a century. Her memory, to the last, was a store of useful knowledge and general information; often have we wished for it in latter years and days of study. She was well versed in the history of nations, and had learned from tradition every important incident connected with our own loved country, from the commencement of Maryland's great part in the historical drama, or from its settlement by the Calverts in 1634. Her experience and personal acquaintance with the leading characters of Virginia, Maryland, etc., would have sufficed for volumes: unfortunately, we knew not the treasure we possessed until it was hopelessly lost.

Grandma had long been promising us a

series of historical facts and anecdotes of the old Colonial period. She one day remarked that as Yule-tide was approaching she would make those stories one of her Christmas-gifts to us; it is needless to say we counted the days and hours and could hardly wait with patience the coming of those joyous evenings when all could be together, free from books and essays.

On the second evening of the glorious festival, we were summoned to the dear old lady's sitting room where we found her prepared to give us a charming welcome. A neat little table in front of her large arm-chair, was laden with knicknacks of all kinds, each bearing the name of the one for whom it was intended. It was a jolly moment, one never to be forgotten.

Well, after the presentation ceremony was over, and many loving words to our grandma, Charlie, the oldest amongst us, became spokesman for the evening and ventured to remind our hostess of the promised stories. He began with: "Now, grandma, let us have a toast to the good olden times of yore, and to your youthful days."

She laughed in replying: "Yes, Charlie, those were good old times; there are none like them now and never will be."

"Grandma," said Charlie, "don't you think every generation says the same? I bet when we are old we shall tell the youngsters about our grand old times, won't we, grandma?" I can just hear myself now telling the little boys and girls about to-night and all the other pleasant evenings you have given us."

"Well, yes," replied grandma, "that is true, but our times were different from any that will ever occur in the future of this country. We were in the midst of war, and the rumors of war, and had a great deal to contend with, anxieties of every kind.

"All, rich and poor, had the same trials and difficulties, and all were united, having one heart and one soul, determined on resisting the oppression of our mother country, England. We had to work and turn our hands to everything and anything; still, we were happy, except when thinking of the dear ones that had fallen on the field of battle, and of those who might share the same sad fate."

Grandma lost two brothers, both under Washington, and she never spoke of them without a sigh or a tear, and no doubt she often wept bitterly in her silent hours and moments. She told us of many that were never heard of after they enlisted.

She was born in 1755, consequently, was ten years old when the famous Stamp Act was passed by the British Parliament in 1765, and could relate many incidents and interesting anecdotes of that perilous age. She told us the Act created great

2

consternation throughout the entire country, and especially among the business
portion of the population, as all the legal or
business paper was stamped and could not
be used without it. In those days a great
many grants, deeds, transfers, etc., had to
be signed by the Lord Proprietary or
Lieutenant Governor, and the cost
amounted to quite a sum, which few could
afford. But the young people did not
bother about the Stamp Act, "for, as
you may imagine," said grandma, laughing,
"our love-letters were not written on the
stamped paper. But when, in the following
year the Act was repealed and the
duty put upon tea, glass, etc., then you
ought to have heard the ladies talk ; old and
young were roused to the highest talking
pitch.   They held meetings of indignation
and drew up resolutions of protest, etc.,
which, however were never sent to King
George or any of his representatives.

"One elderly lady declared she would die without her tea, and that if it was beyond her ability to get it, she would give up the ghost; that tea was her only beverage, and she would become as dry as a haystack if deprived of her little tea-pot. To her dining-room maid she said: 'Minty chile, take good care of the tea; it's going to be taxed, and I do not know if we will ever see any more after the present supply is gone. Dear, dear, what will I do?'

"'What,' said the darkey, 'tacks on tea! Why don't dey say nails at once, and be done with it? *Tacks* on de tea! who eber heard of it. Laws, missus! is de Britishers gwine to be as mean as dat, make us drink *tacks* tea? We is cum to a fine pass, indeed we is, to be drinking dat stuff. Surely Massa George Washingtun ain't gwine to stan' dat!'

"The mistress attempted explanation of the tax, but the darkey knew almost as much as the mistress," said grandma, and she laughed heartily.

"In those days, tea seemed to be the general remedy for all pains and aches; if one had a cold, it was, 'take a cup of hot tea, chile, that will cure you.'

"Yes, tea was considered the staple of life and many were the groans and laments at the prospect of its becoming too expensive for use."

Grandma was full of humorous wit and delighted in the telling amusing anecdotes.

"One day," said she, "old Mrs. Wrigger, who sometimes spun for us, came to see about her work, and as soon as she got in she began her tale of woe.

"'Laws sake!' she said to my mother, 'isn't it awful times, Mrs. N—? I hear Parliament has taken all the stamps off the paper and put them on the tea and glass; dear me! what will we come to next? I believe it will be the death of poor mother;

she just lives on tea. She and me sets by
the tea-pot at breakfast, dinner and supper,
and what she don't take I do, so there's
not a drop left betwixt us. I used to be
inclined to like the Britishers, but can't bide
them now; when people touches tea, they
touches me, and I'm done with 'em forever
and aye. Poor mother sets shaking her
foot ; she looks at the pot and then at me;
but she don't say anything, only says she
to me the other day, says she, "Caddy,
won't we miss the old tea-pot!" Says I to
her, "Oh, mother don't be worrying about
the tea; I'll manage to keep the pot
agoing." '

"My mother kindly told Mrs. Wrigger
to tell her mother she would see to her tea-
pot when the worse would come to the
worse.

" 'There, now,' responded Mrs. Wrigger,
'I knowed you would, and told mother so.
Well, I'm going home much more light-

hearted than when I cum in, good-bye,' and off she went.

"Old Mrs. Dempsey made a great to-do about glass; she was not so fond of tea. Her husband coming in one afternoon, she accosted him with: 'John Dempsey, is it true we are to have a heavy duty on glass?'

" ' It seems so,' replied the old man.

" ' Then,' said she, 'I'll give up, for when a pane breaks, where will we get another?'

" 'Cover it up with sheepskin, Sallie, that's plenty good enough these times.'

" 'Cover the window with sheepskin, John Dempsey? Why, surely, man, you are dreaming. Whoever heard of sheep-skin windows? I tell you, sir, they'll never come into *my* house. Sheepskin windows! Great heavens! I'd sooner have no windows at all.

" 'You forget, John Dempsey, that our Sal and Betsy are both going to turn out in company next winter, and how will it look

for people to be riding up the lane and
seeing our sheepskin windows? You may
laugh as much as you please, man, but I'll
never let sheepskin windows in *my* house.
I'd sooner daub up the walls entirely and
have tallow candles in day time. I
know what I would like to do; I would
take every pane of glass in this house, go
over to England and pitch the whole kit
and bile in old George's face; and as to
the tea, I'd make it boiling hot by the
gallon and pour it down his throat until I'd
see him burst every inch of him; then he'd
know what it is to be putting his old
fingers in our pie, as the saying goes.'

" 'Well, well,' said old Dempsey, 'I never
heard a woman talk and go on like you,
Sal; s'pose you hold on till you feel the
weight of the taxes.'

" 'Hold on, and for what? Just to see
the Redcoat walk in and carry off all we
possess, just because we own a little tea

and some glass? When they sez glass they
mean everything that looks like glass, and
nary a tumbler will be left to drink out
of when company comes. I know them
fellers by heart, John Dempsey, and you
don't.'"

Grandma stopped to take a pinch of
snuff and a sip of water, then related
another anecdote.

"Well, old Mrs. Lyons, the weaveress,
entered one afternoon, and she began with:
'Mrs. N——,' said she to mother, 'don't you
think it a mean thing in the Parliament to
be putting the big stamp from the papers,
to the tea and glass? They might as well
have left it on the papers, don't you think
so? I know it puts me in a fix, for just
one month ago I went and bought six glass
tumblers, the first we ever had; we always
drank out of tin cups and gourds, and I
tell you, Mrs. N——, our gourds are nice
enough to give the king himself, but our

Jane gets airs sometimes and she allowed
we ought to have a few tumblers for company, and I gratified her, but I am determined to sell three of them. I'm sure
three is a plenty for any family like ours,
and since Jim Jinks went to war she never
has more than one youngster to come at a
time. I s'pose you don't want to buy any
more tumblers, do you, Mrs. N— ?' Mother
answered her kindly but negatively, adding:
'Haven't you paid for them, Mrs. Lyons?'
'Laws yes I took over to the store three
dozens of chickens, a dozen ducks and two
pecks of dried apples, and exchanged them
for the tumblers; it's true, they throwed in
a wee bit of sugar and a pint of molasses
in the bargin !' "

"You had many a laugh in those days,
grandma," said my brother Edward, "and
I think the women had a great deal of
spunk, hadn't they?"

"Yes, indeed, child, they had spunk and

pluck to the backbone, and I believe if the women had been called to the field of battle, they would have conquered the enemy sooner than the men. But they were generous; mothers sent off their sons, and sisters urged their brothers to be valiant and courageous, and I tell you. children, we had anxious days though many a little sparkling of fun. Every now and then sad news would reach us and our spirits flagged for a while; then again we'd hear of some great victory on our side, and there would be fine cheering; that's the way in war, you know.

"Once a poor man wretchedly clad, came to our house and said he was from Washington's Army in New York; that he had been sent out on the scout, taken captive by the Indians and kept for several weeks, almost starving; he made his escape one dark night and pushed southward. He gave good tidings of our northern army, but we did not trust him much, fearing he was a spy. Father and mother gave him a night's lodging and meals. Next morning he was ill with what he called 'Camp Fever,' and he died in a few hours. We kept his coming and death profoundly secret ; none of the neighbors knew anything about it for nearly a year.

"In those days, when we were told not to tell a thing we dared not speak of it."

"I bet," said Harry, "it would have been told these times as there are so many girls about."

"Thank you, master Harry," said I, "for your compliment."

"When was the first battle fought, grandma ?" queried Harry.

"Well, you know, child, the Redcoats entered Boston, September 27, 1768. General Gage was sent over with two regiments to make us submit to the English taxation, and he carried a high head from all accounts."

"He ought to have had some of the plucky ladies to deal with, Mrs. Dempsey for instance," said our Charlie.

"And," continued grandma, "you know all the duties except those on tea, glass, etc., were removed in 1767. In 1770, only the tax on tea remained and the British were determined to get *that* out of the Americans, and the Americans just as determined not to pay a cent of it.

"Our men disguised themselves as Indians and in the very face of the British, emptied a whole cargo of tea in Boston Harbor. Wasn't it plucky in them? And in Annapolis they burnt the *Peggy Stewart* and all the tea on board of her, but spared the crew and let them get home the best they could.

"In and about Boston annoying little skirmishes frequently occurred, in most of which our men were whipped; that, however, did not discourage them; on the contrary they rallied with more energy and every man and boy that could muster a gun of any kind, hurried northward.

"The battle of Bunker Hill was fought June 17, 1775, and though we lost, Gen. Howe, then in command of the British, was glad to run into Boston and hide his army. After that battle, Gen. Washington was appointed Commander-in-chief and we all said: 'Now we'll whip the Redcoats,' and sure enough we did.

"Prescott headed our troops at Bunker Hill; he was a good general but not like Washington."

"How did you all get the news so quickly, grandma?" asked Edward.

"Why, child, we had smart messenger-boys and men who rode from town to town conveying the result of each battle or fight. As they passed through the villages, even at night, they shouted out whatever it was they had to report; if favorable, there was great rejoicing, but if disastrous, our faces were long enough for days or until we heard something to cheer us. Little boys were paid for carrying the news to private houses, and if you had been there, Charlie, you would have made a few pennies. Every one was eager to hear and know everything concerning the army.

"I knew one poor little drummer-boy who was shot in two by a cannon-ball at Bunker Hill. He went from our neighborhood; his poor mother never got over his sad death, but was resigned to God's holy will, knowing he died in a glorious cause. She knew he would have fared badly if a prisoner in the hands of the English. Oh, indeed, my dear children, we had a mortal horror of the English soldiers, they were so cruel and so deter-

mined on our submitting to their tyrannical yoke.

"Sometimes in the winter our men would
be allowed a furlough or leave of absence
for a definite time, and we would hear anecdotes and stories worth listening to, some
sad, others joyful, most of them amusing.
Of the last you must hear one that will interest you. During the battle of German-
town, October 4, 1777, when the fight was
hottest. Major Burnet, one of the officers
of Gen. Greene. was shorn of his handsome
cue, by a musket-ball. Gen. Greene per-
ceiving it, said: 'Don't be in a hurry, get
down and save your cue.' The major
followed the advice and regained his hair.
A few minutes after, a shot came whizzing
by and carried off one of the powdered
curls of the general. Burnet could not
resist the temptation to retort on his superior officer and said: 'Don't be in a hurry,
dismount and save your curl.' As the

enemy were in close pursuit, the general
preferred to lose his curl rather than himself and fine horse.

"O, my dear children," continued grandma, "our struggle for liberty was a hard
one, but, thanks to Almighty God, we have
been repaid for our sacrifices. You, my
dear ones, can never know how much you
are indebted to your ancestors for what
you now enjoy. and I trust you may be
able to say to future generations, what I
have so often said to you: 'There are no
times like our good old times.' I think
it is time now for our night prayers, so a
happy good night with pleasant dreams.

"Tomorrow evening I will tell you
something of the Declaration of Independence, and the joy it brought to all hearts."

PART II.

DECLARATION OF INDEPENDENCE AND ITS CELEBRATION.

"MOTHER," said my brother Edward, at the dinner table, "can't you let us have supper a little earlier this evening? Grandma has promised to tell us about the Declaration of Independence, and I know it is going to be jolly."

"Advance supper!" replied mother. "I fear you children are worrying your grandma; you must not forget she is old, and should not be fatigued unnecessarily."

Turning to the waiter, she said: "Advance ten minutes, John. I guess that will give time enough, won't it, children?"

"Yes, and thank you, mother," replied one and all.

3

Brother Charlie said in his dry way:

"I reckon if you had seen grandma last night, mother, you would not call her old; it did my heart good to see her so young. I believe she could have danced the hornpipe."

Papa joined in saying, "Yes, and she is yet worth ten young ones."

Nettie, our little sister, went to pay grandma an afternoon visit and told her we were going to have early supper.

"Early supper," said the old lady, "what's that for? Is anything expected?"

"Why, grandma," said the prattler, "the boys told mother you were going to tell us a jolly story about the 'Declamation of Innopenance,' and they wanted more time."

"Good gracious," replied grandma, "do they expect me to talk all night, the little scamps?"

"And," continued Nettie, "mamma said

we must not worry you, grandma, because
you are so old, and Charlie told her you
were young enough last night to dance the
hornpipe. What's that, grandma?"

"The good-for-nothing fellow," replied
grandma. "Tell him, Nett, I will crack his
head for him. I, young enough to dance
the hornpipe!" and the old lady's laugh
might have been heard outside her room.

The hours sped on and soon brought
supper; when all were fairly in, Nettie accosted Charlie with:

"Ah, master Charlie, you are going to
catch it; grandma says she will quack your
head for saying she was young enough to
dance the hornpipe."

"Did you tell grandma that, you little
vixen?" said Charlie. "I declare, mother,
Nettie is getting to be a real tattler and she
ought to be hauled over; she told grandma the other, day that I said her nose and
chin would soon meet."

"Nettie," said her mother, "you really must not repeat to grandma or anyone else, the little things you hear; after a while everyone will be afraid of you. Now, you needn't go to grandma and say I said this, do you understand?"

Nettie was as pleasant as though she had received no rebuke or chiding, and that is the way all little girls should be when corrected, and never look angry or pout when found fault with.

Well, supper was over and we sat waiting for a summons from grandma; after a while down came her maid to say: "Ole missus is ready for the chillun."

How we scampered up the stairs! There was dear grandma, seated in her large arm-chair, closely wrapped in her little shawl. She kissed us all and after taking a good pinch of snuff said: "What did I promise to tell you to-night?"

"The Declaration of Independence," we all shouted.

"Tell me first," said grandma, "when was Independence declared?"

"The fourth of July, seventeen hundred and seventy-six," answered Charlie.

"Yes," said the old lady, "that was the happiest day America ever saw, decidedly the happiest, and there were great rejoicings, I assure you, children.

"We knew our statesmen were in session, debating the point of freedom, etc. Congress was held in the State House at Philadelphia, for you know we had no fixed capital at that time and it was only in 1800, that the city of Washington became the seat of Government. General Washington laid off and planned the city in 1790, and it was then decided to begin the building of the Capitol. Washington took his ideas from a wheel. He intended the Capitol to represent the

hub, and the radiating avenues the spokes
of the wheel.   And here I must tell you
an anecdote lest I forget it.   When it
was decided to remove the Capital, a
countryman met another and hailed him
with: 'Arrah, and did you hear the news?'

" 'No.' replied his friend. 'and what's up,
tell me. Jim.'

" 'Well,' said the other, 'they are going
to fetch the Capitol from Philadelphy
clean down to Washington, and I tell you,
man, there's going to be game in it.'

"Pshaw, Jim,' shouted Jerry, 'you don't
tell me that: how will they ever do such a
thing.   Why, man, it will take years for
such a job as that, and there'll be no team
left at all, at all, after such a pull and
haul.   'Twill kill every horse and mule in
the country to drag such a big house so
fur.'

" 'Ha, ha, ha,' shouted Jim, 'they ain't
going to fetch the *house*, but only the

goods and chattels : they can't move the State House.'

"'But, you know, Jim, 'capitol' means house, and 'capital' city, so a fellow told me the other day, and you say they are going to fetch the Capitol, and sure that means the house.'

"'I believe you are about right, Jerry,' said Jim, 'and I lay bet on seeing that big house hauled down by horse power. George Washington was a great man.'

"At that time, children, Washington was but a small, insignificant village, with only a few houses and shanties. Georgetown was a much handsomer place, and Bladensburg a very pretty little town; at one time they thought of making it the Capital city. But excuse my digression, and now to the Declaration of Independence again.

"For days we were in the greatest anxiety, fearing some of our men would favor subjection to the English yoke a little while longer. Every Colony had what we now call reporters, standing around the old State House in Philadelphia, to give notice of the decision. Besides, all through the country, there were telegraph stations, not wires as we have at present, but very high poles, and it was agreed that if the decision was in favor, a red flag would be hoisted; if not, a black one.

"There was very little work done those days; every one seemed apprehensive of a great calamity, and we prayed as hard as we could, for it would have been worse than death to hear we were still to be under British rule. Well, on the morning of the fifth of July we heard the firing of guns in every direction, and we hoped all was right, still no news had come to us. The excitement all through the country was simply terrible. At last we saw father coming home, as fast as his horse

could carry him. We all ran out and
surrounded him; he was so overcome that
he could only say, 'Free, free!' We cried
with joy and could do nothing but go
from one to the other saying, ·Glory be to
our men; glory be to Congress,' though our
first act was to kneel down and give
thanks to Almighty God for so watching
over his poor American children."

Grandma was quite overcome and we
sat in silence till Nett broke the spell by
saying: "Grandma, did you fire any
guns?" We were relieved by the laugh
she gave us.

"Why, yes. child, we all had learned
how to shoot, and I fired many a gun.

"But," continued grandma, "there were
some few that did not unite in the rejoicings. I mean the Tories, they looked
black enough, I can tell you."

"Who were the Tories, grandma?" enquired Edward.

"The Tories, my dear," she replied, "were those who desired to remain under the English Government, and those who were for free America were Whigs. There was an old Squire Lee, not far from us, who was a noted Tory: he was a sort of cousin to the famous Light Horse Harry Lee, but unlike him in loving America. He was very wealthy, having brought all his fortune from England and would have gone back if he had lived, so it was said. Well, he had an only daughter, Eliza Lee, who despised American ways. She died of pleurisy some years after the close of the war. When she was taken ill her physician assured her she could be relieved and saved only by bleeding. She said, 'No, indeed, I will never allow one drop of my royal blood to be spilled on American soil.' She died, of course."

"Yes," said Harry, "and spilled the whole of her royal blood and herself in the bargain ; what an old spook she must have been!"

" The next thing," continued grandma. " was to consider and make plans for the due celebration of the fourth of July in the future years. It was decided to make it a legal holiday to perpetuity. The first anniversary, we thought, should be kept with as much pomp as circumstances would permit; meetings were held from time to time to devise means, ways, etc., for the celebration of 1777. The conclusion was to have a barbecued dinner in every district of the country, and a ball at night. Well, such preparations you cannot imagine. Some weeks beforehand, a committee of gentlemen in our district met for the purpose of selecting a delightful grove for our entertainment.

" They found in my father's wood a very suitable spot and at once had it ploughed, rolled and beaten till the ground, for about

a quarter of a mile, was as hard as marble ;
the dancing grounds, especially, were
lovely, and no marbled floor of Italy could
have been smoother and more fit for
dancing. Every family agreed to send
supplies for the table, and you know
barbecue means that all the animals,
poultry, etc., are to be cooked whole, and,
my children, it was a curious sight to see
the long tables set off with lambs, pigs,
chickens, ducks, etc., all looking so life-
like that you might have expected to hear
the pigs squeak or the ducks say quack,
quack, etc. The desserts were very handsome and delicious: we met about ten a.m.
and danced till half-past twelve, then had
dinner which lasted till about two, and after
a short recess we danced again till five,
when we had supper. The children had
their table to themselves in a far off corner,
and the little rogues enjoyed it. The
branches of the trees were so closely inter-

laced, that not a ray of the sun could get in at any hour of the day. The children were sent home about six. We began the ball about eight, danced till twelve, then stopped to take cake and lemonade, resumed the dance and kept it up till broad daylight.

"Now, I must tell you about our dresses. All the ladies agreed to appear in homespun apparel. I made two fine linen dresses for the occasion, and three pairs of sheepskin slippers. One pair I trimmed with blue satin ribbon, another with pink, and the third with white. I danced out the blue trimmed ones before dinner, the pink ones in the afternoon, and the white at night.

" One of my dresses was striped with blue and pink, the other pure white."

"My! grandma, were you not tired to death after all that? " asked Edward.

" No, indeed, child, I could have gone

over the whole again without stopping and without being fatigued. We allowed the domestics to enjoy the remnants of the dinner and supper, so they had their turn the next day and enjoyed it, too. We depended on them for the safe return of the dishes, etc., and not one was broken or lost.

" The frolicking in our district was continued for several weeks. We had sailing parties on the Potomac, fishing parties, dances at night. etc., until I believe some *were* tired. We began to feel that our country was safe and free, though we knew our poor men were still fighting for liberty, and, many a hard battle had they after the Declaration of Independence.

" In 1778. France acknowledged our freedom from England. General Lafayette, you know, came to our relief in April 1777, and he brought over quite a number of well-disciplined Frenchmen, though few are mentioned in history. They were everything to our army. Cornwallis, you know, surrendered to General Washington at Yorktown, Va., October 19, 1781, so we had a long, trying struggle. However, the old ladies that were so terribly worried about the tea and glass, were comparatively at ease. Good Mrs. Dempsey expressed her willingness to depart for a better world. She was never obliged to patch her windows with sheepskin, and I heard her daughters married to her satisfaction and did well. Mrs. Lyons used her six glass tumblers when Jimmy Jinks returned from the war, and they made quite a display on the waiter my mother sent 'our Jane,' for a wedding present.

"After the surrender many of the Red-coats, especially the Hessians, dodged around our place and skulked through the country; they met with very little en-couragement to remain, for we were wishing to see them get out as fast as the ocean could drift them over to their own lands. Our own poor men came back to us destitute of everything but their skin, and many had lost a good portion of that precious article. They soon recuperated and enjoyed for the rest of their lives the peace and liberty so dearly purchased. Many families had to lament the loss of loved ones, but knowing the glorious cause for which they laid down their lives, none could grieve.

"Some other time I may be able to relate a few pleasant events that occured after the Declaration of Independence, but cannot now. as I see poor little Nett is dozing. To-morrow evening you shall hear all about my meeting with General Lafayette and the grand ball he gave in Bladensburg. Good night. my darlings."

PART III

GENERAL LAFAYETTE AND HIS BALL IN BLADENSBURG.

"WELL, children," said grandma, "I promised to tell you about General Lafayette; he was truly a great man. You know he arrived in this country in 1777, and history says he brought over eleven officers; from what we saw, there must have been many well-bred gentlemen among his subordinates. I never beheld finer looking men. You know, also, that Lafayette fitted out the vessel and crew at his own expense, so he must have been a wealthy man and one of influence; he was a marquis in France, and, of course, that means something there. Congress, almost immediately, appointed him to the rank of

4

major-general in our army, and a portion
of our troops were assigned him. The
first battle he engaged in, was that of
Brandywine, and our men were routed.
Toward winter, Washington moved far-
ther down the country and took up his
winter-quarters at Valley Forge; Lafayette
and his portion of the army quartered
around Blandensburg; the officers lodged
at the hotel kept by Colonel Bradford; in
those days, only first class men such as Colonel Bradford, a man of wealth and position
kept first-class hotels. General Lafayette
made himself very agreeable, and as Colonel
Bradford had three handsome and accomplished daughters, Lafayette frequently
slipped into their private parlor, and it
was there I first met him. He was a
grand looking man, tall and graceful, a
fine dancer and good musician; his broken
English often amused us. He told many
interesting anecdotes and incidents of

his country, and we could plainly see
he was in favor of Republicanism. He expressed a great desire to become acquainted
with our American ladies, and said he had
heard much of their beauty, elegance of
manners, etc. At length he proposed to
Colonel Bradford, or asked as a favor that
he would be allowed to give a French ball
in his hotel; of course, the colonel agreed,
and you may imagine the joy and excitement of the ladies, old and young, when it
was made known, and such preparations
for a ball I suppose had never been made
in old times or new.

"In those days few ladies had more than
two silk gowns, but they were very handsome. It was the custom for every lady to
be married in white satin and to have, for
what they called 'the second day's dress,'
a handsome brocaded silk: we do not see
such silks nowadays. I assure you, children, a dress would almost stand alone, so

thick and heavy was the material. The young or unmarried ladies seldom wore silk; taffeta and pongee, both a fine texture or fabric of silk and thread, or silk and worsted, were their fashionable dress-goods, with cambric and muslin of the finest texture, and sometimes very fine linen lawn, though that was considered expensive."

"What did you wear, grandma?" asked Charlie.

"Why, child, I wore a blue taffeta trimmed with white satin, and it was considered a handsome dress. Mrs. Washington wore a brown satin, with pearl necklace and ornaments. She was escorted to the ball by her cousin, Major Fairfax, but would not dance; she said her partner was absent, and there was no enjoyment for her while she knew him to be exposed to the dangers of war. She joined in the promenade and left soon after the supper.

Everything was on the grandest scale; the hall lighted with reflectors and colored lamps inside and outside the house, gave a fairy-like appearance to everything; the scene was enchanting, Lafayette and all the officers wore red velvet coats lined with white satin; the tails of their coats were square and stood out as if stiffened; their waistcoats extended to the hips and showed to perfection the beautiful ruffled shirt bosoms, set off with a diamond or pearl pin. All wore short breeches of a fawn color, either cloth or some other material that we knew not the name of; their long white silk stockings were fastened with gold buckles, and their slippers were of a soft, black kid, fastened also with gilt buckles; in those days the gentlemen's slippers were called pumps. It was the style for both ladies and gentlemen to wear the hair powdered; the gentlemen had long cues tied with ribbon. General

Lafayette wore a bow of white satin on his cue. Many gentlemen kept wigs on hand so as to be always ready for an entertainment. They brushed back their hair that not a strand could be seen by which the color would be known, therefore, some with very black hair wore white wigs and all appeared alike, old and young. The ladies wore long trains to their dresses and when they danced the train or trail, as some called it, was thrown over the left arm. The dance of the times was the minuet and at one of the figures the train was dropped for a series of courtesies; it was a part of the ceremony for the partner to lift the train at the proper time, and I believe the gentlemen made it one of their practices to do it gracefully.

"I have always been so sorry, children," said grandma, "that knee-breeches went out of fashion for the gentlemen, and can truly say I have never since seen a gentle-

man in what *I called* a real, full dress. I have
never liked long trousers and the short
vest. General Lafayette asked, by way of
a compliment, I suppose, to lead off the
ball with Miss Nancy Bradford,* and she
was a suitable partner for him, being handsome and graceful. The supper table was
elaborately set and you must believe me
when I say we drank out of solid gold
wine-cups, all belonging to the French
troops or, I suppose, to the general. The
last dance was after supper, and we
wound up with a slow and graceful promenade, a little different from the entrance
one. You may be sure we had enough to talk
about for months and even to this day.

"As General Lafayette had been anxious
to see the *élite* of American ladies, they in
turn expressed a desire to see the French
officers in full uniform; therefore, Colonel

*Miss Nancy afterward married Major Boarman
of Charles County, Maryland.

Bradford gave an entertainment to which he invited both French and American officers.

"The same ceremony was gone through as for the French ball, and it was worth seeing. All the officers wore full dress, even the *chapeau de bras* and sword. One of the old ladies asked the meaning of *chapeau de bras*, and her daughter told her it meant gilt spurs and copper heels. After the opening promenade, a valet approached each officer to remove his *chapeau de bras* and sword, as it was considered contrary to etiquette to wear them when dancing.

"Mrs. Washington made her appearance when the entertainment was about half over; her escort was Baron de Kalb, one of Lafayette's companions; he had lately come from Valley Forge and gave good tidings of General Washington, though the suffering there had been excessive and not a few had died from the want of clothing and protection from the severity of the season."

"Toward the latter part of February, Mrs. Washington called on the ladies of Virginia and Maryland to assist in collecting clothes and other necessary articles for the poor soldiers in different portions of the northern Colonies. You know, children," continued grandma, "that we had not states then; we formed what they called the United Colonies. Well, we responded to Mrs. Washington's appeal, and soon we had wagon loads that were sent under guards to the appointed places.

"The latter part of that year of 1778, we heard of Lafayette's departure for France, his object being to collect money and whatever he could for dear America. He did not return till 1780, when he rejoined Washington and took part in the fight for American freedom.

"In 1781, Washington, Lafayette and others pushed forward to the southern Colonies. Cornwallis was marauding Virginia and its surroundings and Washington had serious apprehensions. Cornwallis had destroyed about $15,000,000 worth of property and had taken his position at Yorktown. A French fleet under the command of Count de Grasse arrived off the coast of Virginia and remained in the Chesapeake waters awaiting orders from Washington, who directed him to attack the British at Yorktown.

"On the twenty-eighth of September, the combined forces began the bombardment, and Cornwallis, seeing no hope of escape, surrendered to Washington; the capitulation took place October 19th, 1781, a day of real gladness for all Americans, though I told you this before.

"Cornwallis feigned sickness and deputed General O'Hara to meet Washington who showed magnanimity beyond description. The surrender virtually closed the long war with England. The Treaty of Peace was signed at Paris, September 3, 1783, and the British left the country November 25th, following.

"Washington bade farewell to his soldiers soon after and retired to his residence in Virginia, a beautiful place called Mount Vernon. Lafayette and his French companions returned to France, and took a conspicuous part in the awful revolution of 1798. He returned for a social visit to this country in the year 1824, and was received with all the honors due to his merit.

Our country began, after the Declaration of Independence, to recover its losses, and in a few years was on a solid footing, coping with other great nations. I must, another time, tell you something of the ways, customs, and hardships of our colonial days, and maybe you will say you are not sorry for being in the after times, so much easier and in some respects better, though I must adhere to my first saying : 'No times can be like our good old times.' Now, let us have good night, and may God Almighty bless you, my dear children."

PART IV.

MANNERS AND CUSTOMS OF COLONIAL DAYS.

"WELL, now, children, where shall I begin?" said our dear, old grandma.

"Anywhere, grandma, that suits you."

"Then, I will tell you first how we prepared our clothing, and begin with the cotton. We planted the seed in the spring and soon we saw the beautiful green bushes growing as tall, some of them, as Master Charlie or Edward. In the fall, the burrs opened with the frost, and early in the morning we would go out with large baskets to gather the cotton. When dry we picked it, that is, we removed the cot-

ton from the burrs, which was a pleasant
pastime in the long winter nights. You
know the seed of cotton contains an oil,
and when it becomes heated, the cotton is
easily taken off; sometimes we threw the
burrs or seed in the fire when the wood
was burning low. You know we had nothing but wood fires in those days; the
fireplaces were very wide, and andirons
supported the wood. Those in the parlors
were made of highly polished brass; the
beautiful fenders, shovel and tongs, were
also of brass, highly ornamented, and, my
dear children, I know of nothing prettier
than a bright wood fire reflecting its
glowing flames upon everything around: it
was cozy and enchanting.

After the cotton-picking, we generally
had apples and nuts or, perhaps, a taffy-
stew. When several young people gathered
together, they sometimes wound up with a
dance: altogether, we had pleasant even-

ings in those good old times. I must tell
you here a little event that may amuse
you," said grandma, with a little twitch of
mischief in her eye.

"One evening, soon after the marriage
of your father and mother, a few young
people came for tea ; two of the young
ladies came to my room to prepare their
toilette ; one of them* had false curls in
her reticule, and taking them out, she laid
them on the warm hearth to soften the
pomatum, which you know makes the curls
fall more gracefully. Well, I saw them
on the hearth and took them for cotton
burrs ; reaching for a little broom, I swept
them into the fire. When she was ready
for her curls she could not find them
and declared she had put them on the
hearth. I heard her and it immediately

---

*Miss Juliann Bevan, who later became a Sister
of Charity at Emmitsburg and died there many
years ago.

occurred to me that I had swept them in the fire and I told her so. I shall never forget her consternation; she had to appear without her beautifiers that evening."

And grandma seemed to enjoy the joke. "Was she angry, grandma?" asked I.

"Don't know, child; she was polite enough to make the best of it, and I fancied she was just as pretty without her curls, though no beauty by any means.

"After the cotton was picked, we had to card and spin it, then wind it into balls and send it to the weavers. All of us had very pretty cotton dresses with little stripes of blue, or pink, etc. That is sufficient about the cotton, isn't it?" asked grandma.

"Well, now, about the linen; that was made from the flax we grew on the place. It was carded into tow, then spun out on a small wheel, into fine fibres or threads. All the underclothing, sheets, pillow-cases, table-linen, etc., were made from the flax, and it was very interesting work. In fact, everything about farming and domestic employment was charming to those that liked it, and most of the ladies enjoyed it immensely. We all knew how to knit stockings, socks, gloves, etc., and sometimes we knit the underwear for the more advanced in years who needed warmer clothing. I knit my father a full set of everything he required in that line.

"The older gentlemen liked their coats, etc., of white flannel, and a very pretty sort was woven for that purpose. We made our carpets of rags sewed together and wound into large balls, and sometimes we dyed them very bright colors. The red was dyed with sumach berries set with copperas, the black with walnut hulls, and the yellow with peach leaves or saffron ; the saffron plant was largely cultivated, and we used it for its lovely flowers, when arranging the large pots that stood in the fire-places during the summer. The farmers raised all their own grain, and every family had a handmill with which they ground their flour, meal, etc., for common use. We sent much of the wheat to the water-mills and had it ground into fine flour, which we kept for pies, cakes, etc. Rye flour also made very sweet bread for daily use, though corn-meal was the staple for breadstuffs. I must tell you the origin of our nice 'hoe-cakes' and delicious 'johnny-cake.' Lord Calvert, to gain the friendship of the Indians, presented them with many little trinkets; in gratitude they showed the white man how to use the corn-meal. On little griddles they baked what they called 'hoe-cake,' and on long, narrow boards that stood before the fire, they baked the 'johnny-cake' which you all are so fond of, so you see we are indebted to the poor Indians for something.

I believe they were disposed to be very kind to the English people."

" Tell us, grandma, " said Charlie, "how the water-mills were worked. "

" Well, child, there was a large and deep pond or dam of water just ahead of the mill; immensely heavy and thick gates, called 'flood-gates,' were kept down to prevent the water escaping from the dam until it rose high enough to work the wheels. When the miller raised those gates, the rush of water was terrifying and the noise deafening, so that every miller was a very loud and high-toned talker. Whenever you hear a person speaking very loudly or in a boisterous manner, you may ask, as we used to do: 'Is he a miller?' "

" What kind of bonnets did you wear, those days, grandma?" enquired Nettie.

"Beautiful bonnets and hats, my dear, made of platted straw, which we dried ourselves when the wheat and rye were gathered in; we also pegged a sort of material that was very pretty for bonnets. What you call crocheting now, we called pegging; you know the crochet needle has a little hook which we named the peg. Once my brother Sam was going hunting and told me over night he had no gloves to wear and it was very cold. I began to peg a pair about eight o'clock and finished one that night; next morning I was up by times and before breakfast I had the other done; now, wasn't that smart in grandma?

" We felt the want of coffee and tea more than anything else, as we were out of the city limits and often had not the time to send for such things; we generally laid in our groceries in the fall and spring. We supplied the want of coffee by roasting rye or gumbo, and you would be surprised what nice coffee they made. Our salt was procured from persons living near the bay or salt-water rivers. It was manu-factured by evaporation. The farmers raised a great deal of tobacco, which they sold to the neighboring merchants, or ex-changed for useful commodities, such as dry-goods, shoes, etc., though very nearly every family had its own shoemaker and weaver. We lived rather economically, those times, while having an abundance of everything needed for comfort and domes-tic life.

· "There were very few really indigent and all were kind in assisting one another. Certainly we enjoyed great happiness: there was no jealousy about style and fashion that I hear of now-a-days. But there was one serious trouble, my children. We were obliged by English law to contribute to the Protestant minister, the tithes of all we made, and I can tell you, it took the heart out of me to see the wagon-loads of grain, tobacco, etc., going to one so hard on the poor Catholics.

"He was the wealthiest man in the United Colonies; had one child only, said to be a very lovely girl. Professors or teachers were brought from England to cultivate her talents, and she was pronounced accomplished beyond everything ever known before in America.

"It was very usual in those days to hear it said: 'such a one has gone home to England, for this, that and the other.'

"Well, the old minister made very little by his riches. His daughter married a very clever, fast-living gentleman, who, in a few years made way with the fortune, and not a penny is now to be found in the hands of the new generations, nothing that once formed a portion of the plantations, bank stock, etc., so cherished by the domino. Some of the grandchildren still survive, but they are very destitute of this world's goods:

truly, a mark of God's retributive justice, "
and grandma shook her head sorrowfully.

"Grandma," queried my brother Edward,
"why is it that the English people seem
always to have had such an ill feeling to-
wards the Catholics?"

"That is easily accounted for, my dear,"
replied grandma. "Don't you know that
Pope Paul III. refused to annul the marriage of Catherine of Aragon with King
Henry VIII. because our holy Church
forbids divorce? Well, the mighty sover-
eign became very angry with the pope and
declared himself head of the Church in
England, and from that epoch, 1534,
Catholicity has been held in abomination by
the English nation. The Catholic spirit,
however, lingers around the throne and
among the people, notwithstanding the hatred to everything in the Church of Rome."

"Grandma," asked Charlie, "how did
you all travel in those good, olden times?"

"What a question, Charlie," responded grandma. "We had very few carriages, it is true, but we managed to get along pretty well. Many of the *richest* loved to ride on horseback; we had fine horses and our ladies rode gracefully; I wish you could have seen them on the fox-chase. The first carriage or coach brought to the Colonies was owned by the Squire Lee of whom I spoke last night. Some had a very neat little vehicle called 'Carry-all' and a ride in it was always desirable. It held many.

"The would-be lords of creation, or aristocrats, drove the stylish 'gig and tandem;' that meant the gig with two, three, and often four fine horses harnessed in single file to the gig, driven by a coachman in livery, while the proud old lord looked on with contempt at the pedestrians and gallant riders met on the way.

It was really a very handsome sight to

behold several of those brilliant equipages on the road at one time.

"The phæton was also in great vogue among the grandees. It was usually drawn by two horses, though some of the old English potentates revelled in the show of four fine animals, capering to the caprice of the haughty owner.

"Those English nobility were very ostentatious, self-conceited people and as much disliked in the new country as they had been in the old. We often wished them back under their old kings and tyrannical masters.

"Of course, we ceased to contribute to the support of the English Church, after Independence was declared and our men began to make laws to suit the Republic.

"In some years the Catholics could look up, though for a long time a secret persecution went on that could not be controlled or taken hold of. Catholics were regarded as a set of ignorant people, who knew nothing but a few prayers and superstitious practices; unfortunately for them, the larger portion of our population, at that period, were dissenters from Rome, backed in their belief and bigotry by the powers of Great Britain and their own immense wealth, consequently their influence was great.

"For a long time we were not allowed to have Catholic Churches. The divine service was given us at rare intervals and usually in private residences. By degrees our numbers increased, and we were able to construct throughout the district, little chapels here and there, or within twenty miles of each other.

"One priest attended to several churches and by that means we heard holy Mass at least three or four times a year.

"In every congregation there were Catholic homes called the Stations. The pastor

would announce on Sunday the Station he
would be at on a certain day of the week,
and, my dear children, you would have
wondered at the nnmbers of old and infirm
that would arrive by the wagon-load, at the
appointed place. It was my privilege for
years to attend to the service, etc., at
my father's. Long before any of us were
up in the morning, the front yard would be
crowded with men, women, babies and
children of all ages and sizes. It was an
amusing, though edfying spectacle for us to
behold ; sometimes we might well have
selected from the motley crowd, old Father
Noah, his wife, his three sons and three
daughters-in-law; so many looked as if just
out of the ark. When the season was fair,
we erected a temporary altar in the yard
and many times have I seen our good old
pastor go to the wagons that contained the
helpless and aged, and give them the Bread
of Life, with tears streaming from his eyes

at beholding such profound veneration, piety and devotion in that lowly and humble portion of Christ's vineyard.

"The hatred of our dissenting brethren to the Catholic clergy in those times was beyond anything I can now describe ; one instance will give you an idea. The gentlemen of those days were great huntsmen, and, in the hunting season, the farmers usually lowered the fencing for the convenience of hunters. Our holy pastor* found out those short cuts and made use of them, as they saved him many miles' ride in his sick calls. On one occasion he was riding through the field of an inveterate Protestant, not knowing the fencing had been raised. The farmer saw him and knew him to be the priest; calling to his domestics, he ordered the dogs to be loosened and set

---

*Fr. David, afterwards Bishop Coadjutor to the Bishop of Bardstown, Ky., consecrated, August 15, 1819.

upon the track of the man of God. His dogs were considered the most vicious in the neighborhood and the terror of everyone; they were always chained during the day for fear of serious trouble. The animals started off in hot pursuit of the priest, and just as they reached him they stopped, turned back and crouched at the feet of their master, trembling in every limb. The darkeys who were in the field expected to see the holy man torn to pieces ; two of them were Catholics. They all declared that when the dogs were in the act of springing upon the priest, a white figure, the size of a well grown boy, stood by the side of the horse, and the dogs instantly turned and scampered as fast as they could run. The humble servant of God turned back also and on coming up with the farmer, raised his hat and said most apologetically: 'I beg your pardon, Mr. N—, for trespassing on your grounds. I did not know you had raised your fencing.' The farmer, for a wonder, raised his hat to the priest and replied : 'You are at liberty, sir, to pass through my fields whenever it suits you'; then turning to one of his servants, added, 'You be always ready to lower the fencing for this gentleman, and to raise it after he has passed.' That hater of Catholic clergymen was never afterward known to say an unkind word of them. You see, children," continued grandma, "how the Lord watches over His anointed. We cannot have too much reverence for our pastors, and in my day we never met a priest without asking his blessing, but I believe that holy custom, like many others, is dying out among our Catholic people. I hope you will endeavor to keep up such old-time practices and prove yourselves worthy of your saintly ancestors. I will sometime tell you a few pretty traits of the dear and holy Father

David. He came to the lower Maryland Missions in 1792, or early in '93. No priest ever did more good than he, and his name will ever be a household word among the people of our section of the country."

"Grandma," said Nett, "did you have any schools in your old times? I wish we had none."

"Why, my darling, do you want to be a dunce?"

"No," replied the child, "but I do hate schools and books and as to these old academies, I wish I could send them out of the country, indeed, I do."

"You needn't laugh, Mr. Charlie for I know you hate school."

"Who told you that?" said Charlie.

"Why, I heard you say the other day that skating did you a great deal more good than the old college."

"I don't mind school and books so

much," continued Nettie, "but I do not want to be so long away from my canary, and my kitten, and my pug dog."

All laughed at poor Nett's heavy sigh.

"Well," said grandma, "I will tell you something about our schools. In the first place, education in the Colonial days could not be much attended to; facilities were meagre. We managed to learn from our fathers and mothers what they had learned from their parents. Occasionally there would come over among the emigrants or refugees from the Emerald Isle, gentlemen of learning who would be glad to get the position of 'tutor' in private families, or assume the more onerous duties of 'country school-master.' They taught well, though it seems to have been the idea of the times that the mastering of the 'Rule of Three' in *Pike's Arithmetic* and 'Equations' in *Bonnycastle's Algebra* constituted education sufficient for practical life. The children learned to write, not on the beautifully ruled copy books of our modern day, but on a coarse, rough paper, the very sight of which would make our delicate children nervous and their tender-hearted mammas more so.

"Slates and pencils were scarce; the children took them by turns or borrowed from each other. They used small lap-boards,painted white,and their crayons were not the artistic charcoal ones of modern make, but a bit of fire coal, which some of the boys were very skilful in pointing; every clever lad took a pride in keeping his favorite girl supplied with a nice coal pencil, so you see there was real gallantry in the 'Colonial country school.' We learned Latin, which was considered a very essential branch of education; spelling was very much attended to, and I think we were better spellers than some high scholars of the nineteenth century. My

6

dear children, always try to spell correctly."

"Ned wishes to know when steel pens were introduced; well, we read that metallic pens were in use among the ancient Romans, and that one or more were found among the ruins of Pompeii and Herculaneum. Such as I see you have now were introduced only a few years since. *

"But, withal," continued grandma, "our men and women were educated and highly cultivated; I meet very few now-a-days to compare favorably with them."

"Did children have parties in your day, grandma?" asked Nettie.

"Why, yes, my dear, they had very nice ones, but not at night as you all have

---

* The first steel pens used in England were invented by a Mr. Wise, in 1803, and a Mr. Peregrine Williamson, of Baltimore, took out the first patent for manufacturing them in America, in 1810.—*Chamber's Encyclopædia.*

these times. The little visitors were expected to arrive about three p.m. and to leave about six, so that they might be snug in bed by eight."

"Good gracious!" we all exclaimed, "in bed at eight! Why, grandma, that was barbarous. The poor, little children!"

"Indeed," replied grandma, "you would all be healthier and better every way if made to go to bed earlier than you do; I do not believe in children sitting up so. late, or dancing and frolicking at night like the old people; we were not allowed to do it and we were very happy, I assure you. But it is time for me to stop talking; I see Nett is sleepy, so good-night, my darlings and a pleasant rest to you."

PART V.

REMINISCENCES OF OUR WAR WITH ENGLAND, 1812—1814.

IT was a real January evening. After a heavy fall of snow a drizzling rain set in, which rendered travel difficult and out-door exercise impossible, much to the discomfort of our boys, Charlie especially, as he had invited his skating club to meet on our pond. Among his Christmas gifts he had received a pair of patent skates, which we surnamed "Seven League Boots," so rapidly did they carry him over the ice, and he was anxious to show them off.

Mother said to us: "Why don't you get grandma to tell you one of her stories?"

"Sure enough," replied Charlie, "run up, Nett, and sound the old lady, then tell us how the wind blows, and if you get us a story I'll pay you."

"Will you give me a pair of skates?" said Nett.

"No," answered Charlie, "but I will give you some trapped partridges."

"All right," said Nett, and off she tripped to grandma's room.

"Grandma," said Nett, "it is an awful evening and mother says, if such another day comes, she will make the boys hem towels or do some kind of sewing ; they are so tired in the house all day."

"Poor darlings," replied dear grandma, "tell them to come up to me and I will tell them a story."

That was just the thing we wanted.

Down came Nett saying: "All right, grandma says come, come."

One might have thought we had not seen grandma for a week, so joyous was the meeting, though she had dined with us and remained till nearly two o'clock chatting, She usually dined and supped with us, but adhered to her old-time early breakfast, saying that she could not wait for us " lazy boots. "

" Well, " said grandma as we entered, "do you want a story? "

" Yes, indeed, " we exclaimed, and Nett added, " Tell us, grandma, what you promised about the last war with England."

The old lady took out her watch and seeing it was only fifteen minutes of five said she would have sufficient time to give us plenty of talk before the supper bell would ring.

"Can any of you tell me," she said, "what caused the war? " No one answered. " Well " she continued, " the English people never got over our shaking off their yoke, and the acknowledgment of our independence by European nations was a thorn that rancored in their hearts. They lost no chance of showing it, and as they were always fighting with some nation or other, they needed soldiers and everything else, so they had the assurance to attack and search our vessels on the high seas, pretending we had some of their men in our service, and sometimes they carried off not a few and pressed them into their army, or imprisoned them. They also entered our waters and carried away the vessels. All *that* our government would not put up with. They remonstrated in vain; the English became bolder until at last Mr. Madison, our fourth president, declared war against them, June 19th, 1812.

In 1813, we had to fight their troops from Canada, while numberless skirmishes took place on the seas, all of which you must read about in your histories. I will only tell you what occurred in our own section of the country, viz: Maryland.

"Early in 1814, Admiral Cockburn

sailed along the coast of the southern
states and later entered the Chesapeake,
doing all he could to intimidate and annoy
the people.

"On August 17th, he was joined by a
large force of infantry under the celebrated
General Ross, who had come over under
the command of Admiral Cockrane. History says, General Ross landed at Benedict
on the Patuxent River, August 20th,
with a force of 5,000 men, and that Benedict is distant from Washington twenty-
seven miles. That is a mistake, Benedict
cannot be less than forty miles from Washington and Ross did not land so strong a
force at Benedict; only a small party
landed there, the others proceeded up the
Patuxent, some of whom landed at Notting-
ham, a small town below Marlborough; all
the others landed in the vicinity of Marlborough, which is about twenty-seven miles
from Washington. The forces concen-

trated at Marlborough. But I must tell you about those that landed at Benedict. They marched to a small village called Bryantown, five miles from our residence, and about twelve or fifteen miles northwest of Benedict. They halted in the village a day and night. Their conduct there was not very gentlemanly. On the heights, there lived an old lady named McPherson. As she had known some of the ravages of the Revolution, there was not much good feeling in her heart for the Redcoat. When she heard they were ascending the hill leading to her residence, she went out to meet them, (as she said) in her short gown and petticoat, such as old ladies wore in those days. She accosted the general very civilly and enquired what business he had with her. 'We are only reconnoitring, madam,' replied he. 'Have you any sons?'

"'Yes, I have one,' answered Mrs. Mc., 'and he is at the cannon's mouth, ready to put a ball through you or some of your comrades. You have no business on our land; we have never interfered with you and you should have stayed at home, sir.' The general smiled and enquired if she could give them something to eat.

"'Yes,' said the old lady, 'I will give you, in God's name, all I have in my cupboard.' Then calling to Jim, the colored man, she directed him to put out all he could find, after which she invited the soldiers into her house.

"'Whose rifle is that over your door?' queried the general.

"'It was my husband's, sir, and he used it well on your people years ago; it was on his shoulder when he saw your Cornwallis give up to Washington at Yorktown.'

"'I would like to have it,' said the general.

"'You'll take my life first, sir,' said Mrs. McPherson. 'I'll defend it to my last breath and whoever dares to touch it will feel the weight of my arm.' She advanced to the fireplace, took up a strong poker and stationed herself beside the door on which hung the rifle.

" 'You are very plucky,' said the general.

" 'Yes,' she replied, 'and all my people are of the same stamp, and I can tell you, sir, that many of you who have come *in* to fight us will never go *out:* your old carcasses will be left on plucky soil. Just then Uncle Jim entered with the eatables, which he placed on a table.

" 'Good day, uncle,' said the general.

" 'Sarvint, sar,' answered Jim.

" 'Will you come with us, uncle?' asked the general.

" 'No, sar, I'se very well satisfied wid my old missus, and won't leave her; she's good to me.'

" 'How long have you been here, uncle?' said one of the other officers.

" 'Eber since I'se bin born, sar ; de old missus of all riz me, sar.'

" 'You had better come with us, and may be we'll take you whether or no,' said the officer.

" 'Ah, sar,' answered Jim, 'dat trick was played too often by your daddies and grand-daddies in Gineral Washington's war. They took my father and made him tote an old sick Hissian into Virginnie, and dad said he was the heaviest old varmint he eber fetched on his back. But dad was a smart nigger, sar, and he done watch for the comin' of de night, and den he cut sticks and flew from the Britishers, ha, ha, ha.'

" 'So you won't come, then?'

" 'Ah, sar, I know you all too well of old and you ain't a gwine to catch dis nigger asleep. '

"No doubt they found old Jim too smart for their use.

"Mrs. McPherson had a pet monkey

named Jacko. When he saw the Redcoats he ran to the tip-top of a large old oak in the front yard and no persuasion or coaxing could get him down. One of the officers said: 'I'll bring him down.' Crack went his rifle and poor Jacko fell dead on the ground. We may imagine the anger of the old lady. She flew to her dear monkey, took it in her arms and turning to the officer said: 'You scoundrel of a vandal; that shows what you are; what harm did this poor creature do to any of you, you vile rascals. Begone off my plantation. I'm not afraid of any of your kind, and God grant that you, sir, who killed my poor monkey may soon fall as dead as he is now. Go off, every one of you.' They must have been ashamed of the brutality of one of their number, and with a 'good day, madam,' they hurried off.

"Whilst this was going on, Captain Gordon ascended the Potomac. History says

he was very much molested on the banks
of that river. It might be truer to say he
molested the people on those shores, In
the lower part of Charles County, in Maryland, there is a tract of land called Cobb
Neck; it lies between the Potomac and
Wicomico, and as the name is somewhat
historic, I will give you its origin.

"In our early days we had no mint or
coins; after the Declaration of Independence
we would not use the English money.
Traffic was mostly in vogue, that is, one
man would trade cotton for corn, another
give his corn for groceries, etc., etc. They
had, however, bars or rolls of silver of various sizes, the largest being the dollar roll.

"In moulding those bars, little divisions
were made so that each piece could easily be
chopped off as needed. Every piece of the
largest bar was the value of a dollar, and
they were called Cobb-dollars from the man
who suggested the silver bars, etc. With

such dollars that tract of land was purchased by the early settlers, hence the name 'Cobb Neck.'

"There lived in Cobb Neck an old gentleman by the name of Hammersley; he was a descendant of the English and celebrated for his exquisite politeness. It was said he never passed the smallest child without raising his hat and saying: 'good morning,' or 'good afternoon.'

"Once he noticed an opossum crossing his path. He stopped his horse and said to the animal: 'Pass by, Mr. Possum.' After that he was surnamed 'Possum Pass by,'

"His grounds ran to the water's edge of the Potomac, and his residence was but a short distance from the landing. Captain Gordon cast anchor directly opposite Mr. Hammersley's plantation. The old gentleman, seeing several barges filled with Redcoats coming toward his place, proceeded to the landing to give them welcome. He

was most courteous and invited them to his
dwelling, set out wine, etc., and expressed
regret that his madam was not at home to
assist him in offering them hospitality.
They conversed for a length of time and
no allusion was made to the purport of
their visit—plunder. On leaving they
politely thanked Mr. Hammersley for his
courtesy and assured him that nothing on
his place should be disturbed. In almost
every other house in the same section,
everything was lugged off that the men
could lay hold of. The feather beds, pil-
lows, etc., were taken to the windows and
doors, opened with bayonets and every
feather scattered to the winds. The poultry was shot down, the fruit and vegetables
carried away, and every outrage that could
be perpetrated marked their passage
through the neighborhood. Fortunately,
the women, children, servants, horses, etc.,
had been sent into the interior of the coun-

try, and the silver and other valuables secreted in some place of safety.

"Some miles above Mr. Hammersley's, the militia made a desperate stand and a smart skirmish ensued. The British were worsted, then continued their sail to Alexandria, where they loaded their ships with every species of merchandise. On descending the Potomac, they fired several times into Cobb Neck, and, only a few years since, large cannon balls were lying around in the yards of some of the residences. They were of immense weight, and children could roll but not lift them.

"The American forces were concentrated near Washington, and their aim was to keep between the enemy and the Capital. The British wound themselves betwixt the city and the road leading to Baltimore by Bladensburg. They knew reinforcements could join the Americans from that direction. They drew up their lines on a plain

7

near Bladensburg, and the Americans under General Winder, advanced to give battle about noon, August 24. Your father," said grandma, "can tell you more of the fight than I, as he was a surgeon in the marine corps under Commodore Barney.

"Father had just graduated as physician · a few months previous, and when the call was made for troops in Georgetown, where he was at that time, he enlisted and received the appointment of surgeon. He said there was no reason why our men should not have been victorious, and thought they would have been but for the cowardice of their general, Winder, who, when the fight was thickest, galloped off at full speed. Then, of course, the ranks broke and the soldiers began to scamper in all directions. Commodore Barney and his marines fought to the last, and fired backward, when retreating from the enemy, who did not make any endeavor to pursue the fugitives. Father used to say *his* gun was the last fired by the Americans.

"So anxious were the victorious Redcoats to enter the city, that they took no notice of their wounded and dead on the battle-field. Ross entered Washington about eight in the evening. He and his vandals spent the entire night in burning and destroying everything they could lay their hands on. Grandma said the flames of the burning offices and buildings were distinctly seen at her residence, fully forty-five miles below Washington.

"After the battle, father was appointed to visit the grounds and examine the dead and wounded. The loss of the Americans was about eighty ; that of the enemy about two hundred and forty-nine. Among the dead was a handsome young English officer. In his pocket was found a Catholic prayer book, bound in red and gold, and within its leaves, a letter to his wife in England. He told her his commission would expire in three weeks and he would turn homeward, hoping to be with her and his dear little ones in a few months, or just as soon as he could be taken across the ocean. There were marks of tears on his letter, and poor father could never speak of that circumstance without expressing sympathetic regret. Our men buried the enemy's-dead with their own. Ross left Washington on the evening of August 25, and reached his gunboats in the Patuxent River on the 27th.'

"His next appearance was before Baltimore, September 12th. On his march toward the attack, it is said he remarked he would sup in Baltimore or in the lower regions.

"He did not sup in Baltimore, as he was killed by a discharge of cannon about 3 p. m. Some say Ross was fired at from a tree. by two daring boys of Baltimore, who were instantly shattered into atoms by the Redcoats.

"It was on the occasion of the battle of Baltimore, that the far famed "*Star Spangled Banner*" was written by the patriotic Francis S. Key, of Maryland.

"But, my dear children," resumed grandma, "we in lower Maryland were not the only sufferers. The inhabitants of the little town of Havre de Grace, at the head of the Chesapeake, endured indignities and injury almost exceeding ours.

"The ships being so near, the enemy could well load them with their booty ; they ransacked every house and burnt to the ground some of the handsomest dwellings.

"General Parker had command of that division of the English troops, or vandals as they may be truly called. O, my children, war is a terrible scourge. And may none of you ever have experience of it.

"After the defeat at Fort McHenry or Baltimore, the enemy sailed around to New Orleans, where they were met by a superior force under the intrepid General Andrew Jackson. A terrible battle ensued and the British were driven back with great loss. Almost at the beginning of the fight, their leader, General Packenham, fell mortally wounded. That, of course, spread terror among his followers. I think they must have been glad to sail out of the Crescent City, though every hope of conquering the Americans was lost. The eighth of January will ever be a memorable anniversary for the inhabitants of New Orleans.

"Some weeks after, news was received of a definite Treaty of Peace having been signed at Ghent by the American and English commissioners, and you may be sure there was great exultation and rejoicing throughout our immense country: everyone felt safe once more."

"Grandma," asked Edward, "what became of Lord Cornwallis after he surrendered to General Washington? Did he ever return to England?"

"Why, yes, my dear." responded grandma, "he went back and continued to render service to his country for many years. The last notable thing I remember having heard of him was, that he was commissioned to see Napoleon safely landed on the Island of St. Helena, and you may be sure he did *that* duty to perfection, and saw that the poor general would never have it in his power to move a budge from the spot marked out for his last resting place. Poor Napoleon!"

"Was he a good man, grandma?" enquired Charlie.

"Yes, Charlie, he was good in some

respects, and very bad in others. He was raised up by Almighty God for a great work and he accomplished it; had he been content to remain as he was, he might have become one of the greatest men the world ever beheld, but Napoleon was elated by his success and became a proud, ambitious man, desiring to conquer the world, so it was well for his career to be checked before too much mischief was done by him. We all have good and bad qualities, Charlie, and it is necessary for us to be watchful and put to profit our knowledge of them, ever endeavoring to root out the bad and to improve the good, that we may attain the end God had in view in creating us. Another time I may tell you more of some of the noted men whose names you will see in history and other good books. Now, I think, it must be time for us to stop. My watch says it is near seven, the hour for tea."

OUR ANCESTRAL HOMES.

BUSHWOOD,

ST. MARY'S COUNTY, MARYLAND.

THE nineteenth century is drawing to
a close and with its departed sisters
will soon be numbered with "The Ages of the
Past." From the first pages of its Annals
to the last, we can trace the workings of
an all-wise Ruler and His watchful Provi-
dence over our beloved country, thus
proving it to be the land of His adoption
and of His love.

Comparing the close of the century with
its commencement in America, we are lost
in wonder at the complete transformation
of all things around us and read with

laudable pride, the events recorded by history, with the rise and progress of the nation. History, however, has made no mention of the lordly mansions of our ante-Revolution or Colonial days, some few of which still exist and are pointed out as precious landmarks or links connecting the present with the past and future.

It must be remembered that after the settlement of the Colonies, not a few of the English nobility emigrated to our shores, bringing immense wealth, by which they were enabled to maintain or keep up the style and customs of the mother-country. Lavish were they in making their homes and surroundings correspond with their aristocratic ideas. Even after the Declaration of Independence, the descendants of the high-born lords, vaunted their pedigree, displayed their coat of-arms, emblazoned their coaches with heraldic escutcheons and vied with each other in showing the new world some of the pomp and pageantry of the old.

But, it is of their *mansions* we wish to give the rising generations an idea.

Where shall we find them? They are dotted all along the heights of the historic Potomac, on the elevated ridges of the Wicomico and Patuxent rivers and on the lowlands, whose shores are laved by the bays and inlets that so beautifully indent the coast of southern Maryland. In forest districts also, and in the inland sections, we may now and then meet an old homestead, whose historic legends and traditions have never been caught up by pen or pencil, and which no doubt, would throw a vivid light upon the days of yore. It seems to be desirable that some energetic historian or antiquarian, (one with mind unprejudiced against sect or section, creed or 'nation,) would come among the old ruins of our lower counties and gather the

historic points that have rested in oblivion
for centuries; such a gleaner might find
the wherewith to add to his already well
filled volumes, pages that would be read
with interest in every State and Territory
of our Union, or wherever a Marylander
may be found, and such seem to be scattered broadcast throughout the land.

While awaiting that abler pen, we
venture to give a brief sketch of a few of
the old places of Colonial note, and shall
begin with the one most famous in the
history of our State, viz : " BUSHWOOD,"
the home for generations of the Anglo-
American Plowdens.

Bushwood is beautifully situated on an
eminence that slopes to the water's edge
of the Wicomico, quite near its confluence
with the Potomac. The mansion is
strongly built in the old ancestral style of
England and of material imported from the
mother-land. The prospect from the resi-

dence and heights can scarcely be surpassed. For miles the Potomac may be seen winding its way northward toward our grand Metropolis, Washington, at which point it takes its course to the mountains of the northwest, where its tiny source may be found.

Though the river is about eleven miles in width at its junction with the Wicomico, the shores and hills of Virginia are dis tinctively visible from Bushwood. With a strong spy glass, or telescope, the farmer may be seen tilling the soil and the cattle browsing on the green sward above the river.

Directly opposite Bushwood is the historic "Cobb Neck" in Charles Co. ; so low is its situation between the two rivers, that a beholder from the heights is seized with a fear of its sinking below the waters. After a dead level of about six or seven miles, the surface of Cobb

Neck begins a gradual ascent to the
highland above, where the elevations o
the Potomac on the left and those
of the Wicomico on the right, verge
into a dense woodland, usually called
"Picawaxen Forest."

A drive through that forest in spring or
summer is most delightful; the level road
wends for miles in a perfect shade, then
cuts through a pine forest, leaving on either
side a mass of brush and underwood so
dense as to be impenetrable to the rays of
a noonday sun. The monotony of the
drive is tempered by a view, now and
then, of a handsome residence, with its
fields of growing grain, tobacco and the
like. Occasionally, a cleared spot gives
the traveller a glimpse of the Potomac
and the far away Blue Mountains of
Virginia. Birds of every sort and species
flit by and overhead, heedless of the
stranger and fearless of molestation.

Of that beautiful forest, one at Bush-wood has a clear view. In the autumnal months, when the foliage presents every variety of color and shade, we might ask if such a spot is not something beyond the ordinary creation of nature. We can never tire viewing the works of God from the heights of Bushwood.

The earliest mention of this old residence, we find in the history of Bancroft, where it is written: "The first representative assembly emanating from the people was held at Bushwood." It is also said by the same author, "that a resolve as to the ancient coinage of Maryland was made there by the burgesses about the year 1654."

The next mention of Bushwood is met in the will of Gerard Slye, made in the year 1753, in which he bequeaths the half of Bushwood to his son, George Slye, and the other half to his wife, Mary

Slye, during her natural life, with the condition of its going to George Slye at the death of the widow.

Again, in the will of George Slye, made in 1773. Bushwood is bequeathed to his nephew, Edmund Plowden, in case his widow, Clara Slye, dies without heirs; her only child, Mollie Slye, died when seven years of age and, of course, the Bushwood estate accrued to said Edmund Plowden and his heirs.

In the same will of George Slye, his wife, Clara, was bequeathed two acres of land on which stood a chapel, near the residence, Bushwood. The chapel has since risen to the large and handsome Church of the Sacred Heart, which is attended by the Jesuit Fathers of Leonardtown. In the cemetery attached to the church, may be found handsome tombs and flagstones, bearing the names of the Plowden and other families, for generations.

Said George Slye and his sister Henrietta, who married Edmund Plowden, the father of the first owner of Bushwood, were the only surviving children of Gerard Slye, Esq., a man of note and power under the British Government. His estate in Maryland becoming somewhat involved, he made a voyage to England, either to recover property or to attend a lawsuit. As soon as he left America, his wife, Mary Slye, began to curtail expenses, and in seven years, the length of his stay abroad, the estate was cleared of difficulty and she hastened to join him in England. He returned with her and soon after became a Catholic. Their two children, George and Henrietta, were left to the training of the mother, yet, on account of the father being a Protestant and the laws against Roman Catholics so rigid, she was compelled to send them every Sunday to the Protestant Church; the children would

enter the church, make a noise to attract
the attention of the Congregation, then
run to the servants in waiting outside,
and be driven to the Catholic Church,
where their mother was worshipping.
The Slyes lived very handsomely; their
equipage was among the best in the country.   The old English style of livery was
a buckskin suit with brass buttons, a black
hat with gilt band, and high black boots.

A curious fact relative to the daughter,
Henrietta, deserves mention.   She was a
young lady of great beauty and among
her suitors was a nobleman of English
birth.   One night she dreamed she saw
the English lover, with another young
man attired in black, appear before the
judgment-seat of God.   The Englishman
was rejected, and the gentleman in mourn-
ing accepted.   The dream made such an
impression on the mind of Miss Henrietta,
that she discarded the English lover.

Soon after, she met Edmund Plowden, in whom she recognized the stranger of the dream. He proposed and was accepted.

Edmund Plowden, the husband of Henrietta Slye, was the lineal descendant of Sir Edmund Plowden, Earl of New Albion. Sir Edmund Plowden received, in 1634, a Charter from Charles I. of England, the commencement of which runs thus: "To Sir Edmund Plowden, Earl, Knight, Lord Palatine, Proprietary and Governor of New Albion, etc." In another part of the said Charter, Sir Edmund is granted, "four hundred miles of land, lying on the Bay of Delaware, between Virginia and the New England States."

We learn from the old records in St. Mary's county, that a tract of land, consisting of 4,000 acres, was surveyed March 24th, 1650, and the possessor, George Plowden. The tract was called "Resurrection Manor."

Again, a place called "The Tavern,"
consisting of 200 acres, was surveyed
March 20th, 1670, George Plowden, possessor.

" Plowden's Discovery, " granted to
Edmund Plowden, 1746, was devised by
his will, dated 1757, to his son, Francis
Gerard Plowden.

From the many investigations into the
genealogy of the Plowdens, no possible
doubt can exist of the lineal descent of
the American Plowdens from the old Sir
Edmund, Earl, Knight, Lord Palatine and
Governor of the Province of New Albion,
according to the Charter of 1634; nor can
it be denied that the rights, privileges, and
titles by which Sir Edmund was honored,
belonged to his descendants in America,
and had investigation been made by them
at an earlier date than what we have, every
difficulty might have been removed.

The late Most Rev. James Whitfield,

the fourth Archbishop of Baltimore, assured some members of the Plowden family in America, that he was raised and educated in England, in the same neighborhood as the Plowdens, and was intimately acquainted with the family. He saw a striking resemblance in the American Plowdens to those in England.

A few years since, some of the descendants of the Plowden family journeyed to England to obtain important facts relative to their English ancestry. They visited Temple Church, London, to view the tomb where the remains of Sir Edmund Plowden, Jurist, (grandfather of Sir Edmund of Albion,) are entombed in a handsome sarcophagus, surmounted by a life-size figure in effigy, of the noble dead resting beneath.

The Plowdens were connected by marriage and relationship to the leading families of Maryland and Virginia, viz:

the Brents, Neales, Fenwicks, Carrolls, etc.,
and history can tell the services rendered
to State and Church by their worthy
descendants.

We read that after the disturbances of
Clayborne, 1635, Protestantism attained
its ascendancy in Maryland, and that notwithstanding the " Repeal Act, " passed in
1649. the Legislature of Maryland, five
years later, declared the Catholics "not
entitled to the protection of the laws of the
State."

The indignities and insults to which they
were subjected, we have learned from the
traditions handed down by our Catholic
ancestors, as well as from those who were
opposed to our religion.   In 1661, rights
being restored to Lord Baltimore, the
Catholics, for about thirty years, enjoyed
comparative peace, or until the fall of the
Stuart dynasty, 1688.

William of Orange found the English

people but too ready and willing to re-open the blood-stained paths that had been traced in the time of the lawless Henry and his winsome, wily daughter Elizabeth; consequently, the spirit of animosity was again stirred against the Catholics of Maryland and they endured persecution and trials untold, until the Declaration of Independence.

Sir George Slye not being a Catholic at the time accounts for his residence being a rendezvous for the government officials of Maryland. Annapolis was selected for the capital of the State only in 1699.

Edmund Plowden, great grandson of the Earl of Albion, married Jennette Hammersley of St. Mary's Co., December 5th, 1779, and from them our States and Counties have had some of their most distinguished statesmen and citizens of every profession, and too much cannot be said of their noble efforts to sustain the rights and privileges of their countrymen, irrespective of creed or worship. To them, especially, is the Catholic Church in America greatly indebted for their steadfast faith during the turbulent days of prejudiced ascendency, for, certainly, it was not a little encouragement to the more lowly to behold strict adherence to "Roman Catholicity," among the wealthy and influential portion of the struggling Church.

Rev. Charles Plowden, a relative of the owners of Bushwood, was among the early missionaries of lower Maryland, and much has been told of his noble zeal and generosity. He bestowed his large fortune upon the missions and lived in bare sufficiency during his laborious career, far from the comforts of family and home. He returned to Europe when his days were drawing to a close and died in France.

Sir Edmund Plowden, consort of Jennette Hamersley, was registered as a

member of the Maryland Legislature in
1791, and was still there in 1798, six years
previous to his demise, April 20, 1804, his
wife having preceded him to the tomb by
only a few months.

The venerable Mrs. Austin Jenkins, now
residing in Wilmington, Delaware, is the
only surviving member of their third
generation. Though a little over the four-
score of years, her intellect is unimpaired
and her memory clear and retentive. Her
children may well rise up and call her
blessed.

Edmund Plowden, of William, the last
of his race to possess Bushwood, died in
1864. After his demise the beautiful
homestead passed into the hands of
strangers, who are most courteous in pointing out to tourists and visitors every spot
of interest in the mansion and its surroundings. The old Council Hall is still to be
seen and one can but exclaim on entering

it : "Would that walls could speak."

As nations pass away with time and dynasties change, so do we find that of the old influential families of our Colonial days, there is scarcely a member to perpetuate the memory of, or to carry to coming generations the name of his noble ancestors. Truly, a lesson to teach us the vanity and nothingness of all here below, save what has reference to the kingdom of Heaven.

But Bushwood cannot die ; it must live in the heart of the patriot and be cherished for its connection with the history of the early struggle of our nation for the liberty it now boasts of. In the near future there may be found someone to investigate, more closely, the right it has to a prominent place in the general history of our great Republic.

Of those that clustered around the festive board of Bushwood, (whose very name is synonomous with hospitality), but few remain and they are scattered far and near. In the days when the land was filled with peace and plenty, Bushwood was the centre of attraction. 'Twas there that the lord and lady met to trip the light fantastic toe ; to feast on the luxuries of the deep, taken by themselves in their fishing-parties, turtle-hunts, etc. 'Twas there that the needy sought and obtained assistance, that the Catholic missionary found rest and quiet after his arduous duties and fatiguing rides, for then the Catholic missions were few and far between. 'Twas there the neighbor sought consolation and solace in his hour of trial, the wayfarer a refuge from the tempest and the benighted traveller, a home in a strange land.

We will glance once more at the hallowed walls, the deeply recessed windows, the corridors and spacious halls, and all that bespeak the ancient glory of the

historic Bushwood, •then hang upon its
time-honored portals the following tribute
of affection and due appreciation of what
it was in the days of yore and what it will
ever be in history.

The *harp that once thro' Bushwood's halls
  The soul of music shed,
Is hush'd and still within its walls
  As Bushwood's noble dead.

No more will chevalier and knight
  In tilting make their mark,
Nor sportsman hunt the fallow deer
  In Bushwood's lordly park.

The glory of its day is gone,
  And peace be to its Shade,
'Round which the laurels Hist'ry twined
  Will never wilt or fade.

---

*The last harpist of Bushwood was Henrietta
Plowden, daughter of William.

I N lower Maryland, on the heights of the beautiful Potomac, and not very distant from its junction with the waters of the Chesapeake, the old Blenheim mansion peered above the surrounding residences of the picturesque vicinity. It was built in the latter part of the seventeenth century, and was famed for the strength and solidity of its structure. Its owner was Squire Lee, a descendant of one of the Lees who emigrated from England soon after the settlement of Maryland by the Calverts. Not only the mansion but all the out-houses, stables and pigeon-house, were built of brick imported from England for the purpose. Modern builders have asserted that those bricks were made of quite a different material or earth from what has ever been found in our section of North America. The English brick is thoroughly red and hard to break.

The old mansion was a square building, two stories high, with an attic. The roof, for more than half its length and breadth, was arranged for a fish-pond, and it was said that the old Squire actually supplied his table with trout caught by himself in that overhead fishery; no one else was ever allowed to fish there.

The windows of the mansion were most curiously constructed, and consisted of many panes of stained glass, all very small and of different sizes, shapes and colors. When the evening sun reflected its rays upon them, the effect within was enchanting, and dazzling without. The heavy damask curtains added not a little to the beauty of the scene, especially about sunset.

All around the roof was an iron railing,

to prevent accident to those who loved to ascend for the magnificent view there presented. For miles, or as far as the eye could reach, the most beautiful of American forests, the green hills and plains of Virginia, and, on a clear day, the far off Blue Ridge Mountains, formed a panorama that the eye rested upon with delight.

When the old Squire desired to be the perfect Englishman, he invited his visitors and guests to a view of the surrounding country, through his "first class spy-glass," as he termed it. At the south end of the roof, a small tower was erected to protect the instrument, which was kept mounted, except in bad weather, then there would be quite a ceremony of calling in two or three stalwart darkeys to aid in lowering a movable covering for the " dear telescope." Viewed through the instrument, the scene at night was one of grandeur, especially in the autumnal months, when Orion, Taurus, and the sister constellations appear in their glory. It was the Squire's greatest pleas-ure to watch and note the rising, the cul-mination and the setting of the stars, and when the nights were cloudy, he was sure to be in a disagreeable mood.

He delighted also in fox-hunting, and his hounds were generally pronounced the best in the country. When he heard them praised his usual comment was: "English blood in them." Many a brush did he send to his friends "at home," as England was often called in those days.

He kept a set of handsome barges for crossing the Potomac, to visit his clan in Virginia. Occasionally he gave magnifi-cent entertainments, all on the English plan and in the English style. We never heard of the old Squire having any sons; we only know of two daughters, one of whom survived him. If noblemen could have been hooked as easily as the trout in the father's skyey pond, they might not have died wailing their single blessedness.

The Squire was on intimate terms with General Washington, and they frequently exchanged visits. After the first inauguration, he tendered a grand banquet to the President. Ladies and gentlemen, from far and near, attended in full colonial costume and it was said that the head-dress of the hostess towered fully a foot above her powdered hair. The best band of music that New York could boast of, was hired for the occasion at an enormous expense. The dance was kept up from nine in the evening to near dawn.

Washington and many other Virginians attended the funereal rites of the old Squire. The service was performed by the then leading minister of the Church of England, the old Domino Campbell. His eulogy was long and gratifying to the family and friends.

It was the custom of all the old English settlers to have their burial-ground quite near to, and within sight of the family residence. Every individual grave was surrounded by a brick wall about three or four feet in height and covered with a massive flagstone of the best marble, on which were engraved the name of the deceased, his age, date of emigration and demise. All the slabs were imported from Europe, and sometimes it was years before the last resting place of a dear one was completed.

The last survivor of the old Squire, Eliza Lee, died soon after the close of the Revolutionary War, or about 1792. Before breathing her last, she confided to a very special friend the secret of having in her possession a bag of gold coin, which she requested should be placed umder her head in the coffin, and buried with her. The promise seems to have been made, but how kept we do not know. It is certain that a bag of something went with her remains to the brick-walled sepulchre and was safely deposited beneath the powdered hair and fine ornaments that—decorated Miss Eliza's seat of knowledge—her royal head.

Such a wonderful secret was hard to keep and we are not surprised to hear it was the talk of the neighboring counties within three days after the royal decease. As the sepulchre had not yet been hermetically sealed, and the expensive flagstone not at hand, two darkeys ventured in search of the gold on the second night after burial. A little after twelve they started and advanced toward the grave with cautious steps ; the small lantern they carried gave very poor light and they were careful to keep the dark side turned toward the mansion. They quietly removed the temporary stone, lifted the royal remains and drew forth the coveted prize, then gently laid the dame to rest again, and replaced the stone.

"Aren't we the lucky fellows," said Jim to Josh, "to be gittin' dat ole squire's fortune and de ole witch's cash. Hurrah!"

"Jump up here," said Josh, " and let us frustricate it," and they mounted a tombstone.

Josh, giving the bag a shake, said :

"Dars no jingle in dis bag, Jim."

"O," replied Jim, "dat's bekase its Inglish gool, and dat don't jingle you know ; let's be at it."

The bag was sewn together with very strong thread, that rendered it more difficult to open than was the grave or coffin.

"Well, come ; you pull one ob de strings, Jim, and I'll pull de oder," said Josh, "and see who gits it ajar de fust."

"Stop, Josh," said Jim. "What's you gwine to do wid de money when you gits it?"

"I'll hide it fust, and arter dat I'm gwine to buy a hoss and cart for Judy and de chillun to ride in of a Saunday," answered Josh, "and what's you gwine to do wid yourn?"

"O, I'se a gwine to git a plantation to raise taters on and not be beholding to de white folks any longer. Ain't dat a gittin up in de world?"

"Come, let's begin de *opperation* and be done with it ; you pull one end ob de string, Jim, and I pulls de oder. Here goes it, we'll open together Jim, pull away."

The bag flew open and lo! Instead of gold, hickory nuts and black walnuts tumbled out on the tombstone.

"Whew, whew! ain't dis a spilt job, Josh?" said Jim.

Their white eyeballs might have been seen at quite a distance ; they looked on with wide opened jaws and knew not what to think or say; their hopes were dashed to the ground, Josh scratched his head and after considering a while, both roared out in a loud laugh.

"Well," said Jim, "let's make de best of de bargin and eat the nuts."

In those days the darkies were very apt in impromptu songs and had great facility in putting their words to music. By the following week a very lively song was going the rounds in the neighborhood, and soon became very popular. It ran thus:

Miss Liza Lee, Miss Liza Lee, your gold is turned
    to nuts,
We'll crack and eat, den fling the hulls into de
    ole cart ruts
Miss Liza Lee, Miss Liza Lee, we wonder where's
    you now;
We guess if you'd come top agin you'd raise a
    dandy row.
Miss Liza Lee, you'd better stay jist down dar
    whar you is,
Kase he dat's got your bag of gold will always
    sware it's his.

The darkeys cracked nuts and ate until near day-break. For a few days they kept very quiet, fearing the white folks would get wind of the robbery and have them arraigned before the court of justice. However, the rumor got afloat that Miss Lee was up every night about twelve, sitting on her tombstone cracking nuts, and so strong was the belief that for years no darkey would pass within gunshot of the old graveyard after night fall. Only a few years since it was pointed out to the visiting tourist as a dangerous spot. At one time the old mansion was said to be haunted also, and various were the tales and stories of hobgoblins dwelling therein.

Report said no one ever returned who had been seen to enter the house or go near it after sunset. Noises were heard, groans, etc., even in broad daylight; everyone shunned the place. At length five young gentlemen determined to as-

certain what the trouble was and to lay
the ghost, if any there were. According-
ly, they went to pass a night in the old
mansion, taking with them rifles, pis-
tols, some bottles of wine, etc. About
eleven they heard the drawing back of
a bolt on the door leading from the cellar
below. They secreted themselves so as
not to be seen. After a few minutes
a huge darkey emerged from be-hind
the door and advanced too far into
the room to retreat before being seized.
He was terrified and at the pistol's point
gave his history. He was a poor fugi-
tive slave from Virginia, and with five
others had been living in the old mansion
for nearly two years. At night they went
out foraging for food, etc., and during
the day uttered groans, etc., that they
knew would frighten off visitors. He
declared they were perfectly harmless and
if the gentlemen would allow it, he would

call his companions and let them speak
for themselves.

The gentlemen saw the poor, frightened
fugitives and believed their sad story.
They advised the darkeys to make their
way out of the county as quickly as possible ; gave them money and clothing, and
kept watch over the old residence until
they knew it was vacated. Many years
after, one of the gentlemen was travelling
in New York State and met one of his old
friends at a hotel. The waiter made himself known to his kind liberator, and
could not do enough for him during his
stay at the hotel. He said the other five
were doing well in the country, and had
often wondered how their kind friends
were, or if they had survived the Civil
War, etc.

When the writer last visited Blenheim,
the lower rooms only were fit for habitation
and they were occupied by mulattoes.

The beautiful and curious winding stairs leading to the story above, and where the old relics were kept, were so rickety that it was unsafe to attempt ascent.

The most noted of the relics was a coach, said to have been the first brought to the United States, or Colonies, The entire body of the vehicle was a bright yellow ; the upper parts of black leather ; the coachman's seat much lower than the seats within. There were, also, several old style chairs, quite unlike any we see in the present day.

But ; alas for Blenheim ! During the Civil War of 1861-1864, the time-honored mansion was razed to the ground by the Unionists. All the beautiful bricks, each of which could have told a tale of the past, were carried off for the purpose of building ovens, etc., at the places of rendezvous on the shores and banks of the Potomac, and for what other uses they were needed. It is said that many of the bricks were sold to the darkeys, or given to them in reward for the service they rendered to the portions of the army scattered in different sections of the county during the winter months. Such a dilapidation and such destruction of an old, historic residence can but call forth the exclamation : *"Sic transit gloria mundi."*

www.ingramcontent.com/pod-product-compliance
Lightning Source LLC
Chambersburg PA
CBHW020749020726
47495CB00008B/2357